Sam the Man & the Secret Detective Club Plan

Also by Frances O'Roark Dowell

Anybody Shining
Chicken Boy
Dovey Coe
Falling In
The Second Life of Abigail Walker
Shooting the Moon
Ten Miles Past Normal
Trouble the Water
Where I'd Like to Be

The Secret Language of Girls Trilogy
The Secret Language of Girls
The Kind of Friends We Used to Be
The Sound of Your Voice, Only Really Far Away

From the Highly Scientific Notebooks of
Phineas L. MacGuire
Phineas L. MacGuire . . . Blasts Off!
Phineas L. MacGuire . . . Erupts!
Phineas L. MacGuire . . . Gets Cooking!
Phineas L. MacGuire . . . Gets Slimed!

The Sam the Man series
#1: *Sam the Man & the Chicken Plan*
#2: *Sam the Man & the Rutabaga Plan*
#3: *Sam the Man & the Dragon Van Plan*
#4: *Sam the Man & the Secret Detective Club Plan*
#5: *Sam the Man & the Cell Phone Plan*

SAM THE MAN 4:

SAM THE MAN

& the Secret Detective Club Plan

FRANCES O'ROARK DOWELL

Illustrated by **Amy June Bates**

A Caitlyn Dlouhy Book

 Atheneum Books for Young Readers
New York London Toronto Sydney New Delhi

$\mathcal{A}$
atheneum

ATHENEUM BOOKS FOR YOUNG READERS
An imprint of Simon & Schuster Children's Publishing Division
1230 Avenue of the Americas, New York, New York 10020

ATHENEUM BOOKS FOR YOUNG READERS is a registered trademark of Simon & Schuster, Inc. Atheneum logo is a trademark of Simon & Schuster, Inc.
For information about special discounts for bulk purchases, please contact Simon & Schuster Special Sales at 1-866-506-1949 or business@simonandschuster.com.
The Simon & Schuster Speakers Bureau can bring authors to your live event. For more information or to book an event, contact the Simon & Schuster Speakers Bureau at 1-866-248-3049 or visit our website at www.simonspeakers.com.
Also available in an Atheneum Books for Young Readers hardcover edition
Book design by Sonia Chaghatzbanian and Irene Metaxatos
The text for this book was set in New Century Schoolbook LT Std.
The illustrations for this book were rendered in pencil.
Manufactured in the United States of America
0819 MTN
First Atheneum Books for Young Readers paperback edition September 2019
10 9 8 7 6 5 4 3 2 1
CIP data for this book is available from the Library of Congress
ISBN 978-1-5344-1258-3 (hc)
ISBN 978-1-5344-1259-0 (pbk)
ISBN 978-1-5344-1260-6 (eBook)

To Xyrell Goldston, Star Reader and
All-Around Good Guy

—F. O. D.

To Xyven and Sean and
"The case of Mom's missing cheese puffs"

—A. J. B.

Sam the Man & the Secret Detective Club Plan

Chapter One

Sam the Detective Man

Sam Graham was a mystery man.

Doing detective work had never been his plan, but when his sister lost her sock, Sam discovered he had a talent for figuring things out.

The sock had pink and purple stripes. Annabelle had looked for it under her bed and behind the dryer and inside her book bag, but the sock was nowhere to be found.

"Did you check your sock drawer?" Sam had asked when they discussed the case at the dinner table.

"Of course I checked my sock drawer," Annabelle said. "That was the first place I looked."

Sam thought about this for a moment. "Did you check every sock ball in your sock drawer? It was Dad's week to fold the laundry, and he always makes sock balls out of the socks."

"It's the best way to keep socks together," Sam's dad said.

Sam pointed a broccoli stalk at his dad. "But this week when you folded the laundry you were watching TV at the same time, right?"

"That's right," Sam's dad said. "The Monday-night football game was on. But what's that got to do with anything?"

"You always fold stuff in the same order," Sam explained. "Shirts, pants, T-shirts, underwear, socks. By the time you get to socks, I bet you're pretty bored."

Sam's dad shrugged. "Sure, I guess you could say that."

"Plus, you were pretty into the football game by then, am I right?" Sam asked.

"You are indeed right, Sam the Man," his dad replied.

"Okay," Sam said. "Here's my idea. You accidentally made a sock ball out of socks that didn't match. I bet if Annabelle went through her sock balls, she'd find her pink-and-purple–striped sock. You can only see the outside sock of a sock ball. The missing sock could be an inside sock."

"I'll go check," Annabelle said.

Two minutes later, she came down-stairs waving a pink-and-purple–striped sock. "Sherlock Sam was right! Dad mixed up the socks."

Sam's dad smiled. "Very smart, Sam the Man. But what about the first sock—I mean the pink-and-purple–striped sock that wasn't lost? Why wasn't it in a mis-matched sock ball too?"

"That's easy," Annabelle said, sitting back down at the table. "I never wash it. It's my lucky sock, and if I washed it, all of its good luck would get rinsed out."

"You never wash it?" Sam's mom asked. "As in *never ever*?"

"Never ever," Annabelle said. "I depend on that sock."

She turned to Sam. "You're a good detective. You should start your own detective agency."

That sounded like a good plan to Sam. Maybe he could even charge money for solving mysteries. If he started a club for detectives, they could work on a lot of cases at once. That way they could make lots of money and also maybe get a little bit famous.

Sam liked the idea of being rich and a little bit famous.

Walking to the bus stop on Monday morning, Sam decided to ask his best friend, Gavin, about starting a detective club together.

"I don't know," Gavin said after they'd gotten on the bus and Sam had explained his plan. "I mean, I like the idea of being a detective. But finding missing socks doesn't sound very exciting to me."

"We'd work on bigger cases than that," Sam said. "Stuff like stolen diamonds and kidnapped cats. It'll be great."

"Kidnapped cats?" Gavin said. "When has anyone ever kidnapped a cat?"

Sam scrambled to come up with a better example of a mystery they could solve. "Okay, what about that time last year when someone stole Miss Fran's coffee cup and it was never found?"

Miss Fran was their art teacher. She'd been very sad about her missing coffee cup.

Gavin remembered. "Yeah, that cup had a picture of her dog on it. She was really upset."

"If we'd had a detective club, we could have cracked that case," Sam argued. "We could have saved Miss Fran's coffee cup!"

"I've always wanted to be in a club," Gavin said, and Sam could tell he was getting convinced. "That's the problem with second grade, in my opinion—there aren't any clubs. Well, unless you count the Clean Hands Before Lunch Club, which I don't."

"We could have other people in our club too," Sam said. "I think we need at least four people to be a real club."

Gavin thought about this. "But what kind of people? Some people I know would make terrible detectives. Like Morris Branch. Any time we have to take our shoes off for PE, he can never find them later."

"Or Rosie Schute," Sam added. "She

always gets lost from the group when we go on field trips. I think detectives should be able to find their group at the zoo."

"Okay, we need a list of what a good detective should be like," Gavin said, pulling a notebook and a pencil out of his backpack. "First of all, they should be good at figuring out clues."

Sam nodded. "And they should just— know stuff, I guess."

"They should be able to make good guesses!" Gavin said, writing in his notebook. "Guessing good is important. Also, they need to be good at writing things down."

"And asking questions," Sam said.

Gavin nodded. "That's a lot of stuff detectives need to be good at. So who do you think we should ask?"

"I'm not sure about everyone yet exactly," Sam said. "But I know who we should start with."

"Who?" Gavin asked.

"The smartest person in our class, of course," Sam said.

"That makes sense," Gavin said. "Are you thinking who I'm thinking?"

The bus pulled up in front of the school. Sam stood and picked up his backpack. "I bet I am," he said. "So let's go ask."

Chapter Two

The Hard Kind of Puzzles

Emily Early was sitting at her desk in Mr. Pell's second-grade classroom. She was reading a book about birds.

Emily Early was always reading books about birds. Looking at birds was her hobby, and she probably knew more about birds than anyone else in the whole school.

"What's the best way to ask her?" Gavin whispered to Sam as they walked into the classroom. "Should we tell her she'll get a prize for joining? You know, a detective club T-shirt or something?"

Sam shook his head. "I think we should just tell her why we think she would like our club."

"She'd like it because she's smart, right?" Gavin asked.

"Sort of," Sam said. "Solving mysteries is like doing puzzles, and doing puzzles is something really smart people like to do."

"I'm only above-average smart, but I like doing puzzles," Gavin said.

"You like doing big-piece jigsaw puzzles," Sam pointed out. "I'm talking about puzzles that are hard."

"Oh, you meant *hard* puzzles," Gavin said. "I get it now."

Emily looked up and smiled when Sam and Gavin reached her desk. "Have you ever seen a picture of a greater prairie chicken?" she asked them. "It has feathers sticking up from its head that look like bunny ears."

"That's cool!" Gavin said. "I wish I had those!"

"Have you ever seen a greater prairie chicken in real life?" Sam asked.

"They're very rare," Emily said. "But maybe one day I'll get lucky."

"You could be a prairie chicken detective!" Gavin said. "And if you join our club, we could help you!"

"We're starting a detective club," Sam explained. "To solve mysteries. We were wondering if you wanted to join."

"Because you're so smart and everything," Gavin added.

"No one's ever asked me to be in a club

before," Emily said, sounding surprised. "Who else is a member?"

"Just us so far," Sam said. "We're still deciding who to ask besides you."

"You asked me first?" Emily's cheeks turned red.

"Of course," Gavin said.

"So are you in?" Sam asked.

Emily nodded. "I'm in."

Gavin high-fived her. "Excellent! Let's meet at recess and decide who else to ask."

"That sounds like a plan," said Sam.

Emily grinned. "I like making plans."

"Sam's the champion plan-maker," Gavin told Emily, and Sam gave a shrug. It was true: Sam Graham was the best at making plans.

But who was best at everything else?

◉ ◉ ◉

Sam, Gavin, and Emily met by the monkey bars at recess. Emily pulled out a little square of paper from her pocket and unfolded it. "I've been working on some ideas about who to ask to join our club," she said. "First I think we should ask someone with good handwriting to take notes on our cases."

"I have terrible handwriting," Gavin said. "But that's okay, because I can just type stuff up on the computer."

"But we won't always have a computer with us when we're working on a case," Sam said. "In fact, we probably hardly ever will."

"That's my point," Emily said. "But it would be good if someone could carry a notebook and write stuff down. In my opinion, Marja has the best handwriting in our class."

"She does really good *G*s," Gavin agreed. "I like someone who can do a good *G*."

"Plus, she has binoculars," Emily said. "It's always good to have a pair of binoculars when you're looking for things. So that would be another good reason to have her in our club."

"Okay, let's ask Marja," Sam said. "We also could use someone who's really good at math. Math people are good at figuring things out."

"Rashid!" Gavin and Emily said at the same time. Rashid was the best math person in their class. He could subtract numbers like seventeen-minus-six without even blinking.

"And someone who's really strong,"

Gavin added. "In case a bad guy tries to beat us up."

"I don't think we're going to do cases with bad guys in them," Sam said. At least he hoped not.

"Well, what if we're working on a case where we're looking for a lost dog, and we finally find it but it's really big and nobody but a superstrong person could pick it up?" Gavin asked.

"Someone strong could come in handy for lots of reasons," Emily said, "especially if they're tall too."

"I think we should ask Will," Gavin said. "He's the best athlete and the second-tallest person in our class."

"Plus, people like him," Emily pointed out. "He would be good at getting suspects to spill their secrets."

Sam thought that figuring out who to ask to join their club was almost like solving their first mystery. It was fun to solve mysteries with other people, he decided. It was like having a computer made out of a bunch of brains stuck together.

"I think we should write Marja, Rashid, and Will letters to ask them to join," Emily said. "We can give them their letters in the morning, and if they want to be in our club, they could meet us at the monkey bars at recess."

Gavin jumped up and down. "I'll write the letters! I'll do it on the computer so that they look official!"

"Now all we need to decide is where to meet," Sam told Gavin and Emily. "Every club needs a meeting place."

"How about here on the playground?" Emily suggested.

Sam shook his head. "We should probably meet where no one can hear us when we're talking about clues, in case they're top secret."

Gavin raised his hand. "Like maybe a closet?"

"Too small," Sam said.

The bell rang for the end of recess. "I can't think of any place," Emily said as they walked back to Mr. Pell's class.

"I'm out of ideas too," Gavin said.

"Me too," Sam had to admit. "I guess we have a mystery to solve."

"We do?" Gavin looked confused. "What is it?"

"The mystery of where our club should meet," Sam said.

"Ahh," Gavin said. "That's a good mystery. But how are we going to solve it?"

Sam stood up straight, trying his best to look like a professional detective. "I'm not sure," he said. "But I know someone who can help."

Chapter Three

The Clubhouse Plan

After Sam got home from school and ate two frozen waffles and drank a glass of orange juice, he went across the street to pick up his neighbor Mr. Stockfish. Every afternoon, he and Mr. Stockfish visited their chickens in Mrs. Kerner's backyard. It was a walk that would have taken Sam three minutes by himself, but Mr. Stockfish liked to move at a very slow pace, so together it took them at least ten.

"I thought about having our meetings at the chicken coop," Sam said after he told Mr. Stockfish about the detective club plan. "But chickens can be pretty noisy. Plus, Gavin is the only club member besides me who lives in this neighborhood. So people would have to get their moms to drive them, and then the moms would probably want to bring snacks to the club meetings."

"What's wrong with snacks?" Mr. Stockfish asked, stopping to examine a bush. "I thought that second graders loved snacks."

"It's not really the snacks," Sam said. "The problem is the moms. They'd probably want to organize everything and make all the rules. I don't want it to be the kind of club where moms are in charge. I want the kids to be in charge."

Mr. Stockfish thought about this. "How many kids are we talking about?"

Sam added it up in his head. If everyone they asked to join said yes, there would be Gavin, Will, Rashid, Emily, and Marja.

"Five people," Sam reported. "No, make that six. I forgot to add me."

"That's a good size for a club—not too big, not too small," Mr. Stockfish said with a nod of approval. "Have you thought about having the meetings at school?"

"We want the meetings to be sort of secret," Sam explained. "It's hard to be secret at school."

"Sometimes the best secrets are hidden in plain sight," Mr. Stockfish said, sounding mysterious.

"I don't even know what that means," said Sam.

Mr. Stockfish leaned down to examine a pile of twigs and dry grass on the sidewalk. "What if you and your friends pretended to be a different kind of club? You could say you were a book club. My daughter Judy has a book club that meets at our house every three weeks. No one ever talks about books though."

"So you're saying that maybe they're not a book club at all? Maybe they're actually a detective club?"

"It's possible," Mr. Stockfish said. He scooped up the pile of twigs and dry grass and showed it to Sam. "Just as it's possible this is an old robin's nest. Actually, this *is* a robin's nest."

Sam looked at the nest. He thought it was neat that Mr. Stockfish knew what kind of bird it belonged to. Sam wondered

if Mr. Stockfish was a bird-watcher like Emily Early. Emily spent every weekend going on bird-watching trips with her family. She kept a list of every kind of bird she'd ever seen. She should probably start a bird-watching club—

Wait a minute.

Sam the Man had come up with a plan.

"I don't think anyone would believe us if we said we were a book club," Sam told Mr. Stockfish. "But we could say we were a bird-watching club and everyone would believe it. Emily, who's in our club? She's a bird-watching fanatic."

"And since you're a known chicken fanatic, no one will think it strange you've branched out to other winged creatures," Mr. Stockfish said, laying the nest on the grass.

"I don't think I'm a chicken fanatic,"

Sam said. "I just like chickens a lot."

"There are worse things to like," Mr. Stockfish said. "Speaking of chickens, I hear our little flock now."

They'd arrived at the top of Mrs. Kerner's driveway. Sam could hear the chickens clucking and clacking. As he and Mr. Stockfish walked toward the backyard, he wondered if Mrs. Haynie, the school librarian, would let them hold meetings in the library at recess, especially if they said they were a bird-watching club. He bet librarians loved bird-watching clubs. He could ask Mrs. Haynie to help them research different birds, so no one would get suspicious and figure out they were really a detective club, especially not Mrs. Haynie.

Hiding in plain sight. It sounded like a plan to Sam.

Chapter Four

The World's Best Detective Club

The next day Sam and Gavin got off the school bus and hurried to their classroom. When they got there, Gavin pulled out three envelopes from his backpack. "We'll know by recess if they want to join or not," he said. "The letter I wrote is pretty good, so I bet they'll say yes."

"Then once we have all our club members, we could go to the library and ask Mrs. Haynie if we can hold our meetings there," Sam said. He had told Gavin his library idea on the bus ride to school.

"Our bird-watching club meetings!" Gavin said, giggling. "We'll promise to be be quiet as mice. Wait a minute—do birds eat mice?"

"I think owls do," Sam said.

"That could be a problem," Gavin said. "Maybe we should promise to be quiet as lizards. Owls don't eat lizards, do they?"

"I think we should be quiet now," Sam said. "For practice."

Sam grabbed the envelope that said *Rashid* on it and took it over to Rashid's desk. Rashid wasn't there yet, so Sam put the envelope on his seat. Even if Rashid didn't see it when he sat down, he would feel it. Sam had sat on an envelope once and wriggled and squirmed all the way through dinner until he realized there was something under his bottom. Envelopes, it turned out, could be surprisingly uncomfortable.

After they'd delivered the three envelopes, Sam sat down at his own desk and pulled out his spelling book. But he couldn't concentrate because he wanted to see Rashid, Will, and Marja open their envelopes. Would they be excited to join a club? Would they want to be detectives? What if they said no, that this sounded like the stupidest club ever?

It had never occurred to Sam that anyone would think his club was stupid. He started to chew on his pencil, which is what he did whenever an idea made him nervous. Maybe he should have talked to Annabelle first. She knew a lot more than he did about what was stupid and what wasn't.

Just when Sam was starting to think that his stomach hurt and he might need to go to the bathroom, Will turned around in his seat, which was three desks up and two desks over from Sam's, and gave him the thumbs-up sign. *See you at recess,* Will mouthed without actually making any sound.

Sam's stomach stopped hurting. Even if Rashid and Marja said no, Will had said yes. That meant they would have four people in their club. And once they got rich from solving mysteries, Rashid and Marja would be sorry they said no. They'd be begging Sam to let them join.

Well, maybe Sam would, maybe he wouldn't. It would depend on what kind of mood he was in.

Walking outside for recess, Sam felt nervous again, but in a good way. He bet that if Will wanted to join their club, Marja and Rashid would too. Halfway across the blacktop he looked over and saw a group of people standing by the monkey bars. There was Gavin, Emily, and Will—and Rashid and Marja! But that's only five people, Sam thought. Weren't there supposed to be six?

Oh, yeah—he was the sixth, Sam realized, running to the monkey bars. He kept forgetting that.

"Everybody's in!" Gavin called as Sam got close. "Now we're trying to decide on a name."

"How about the Ace Detective Club," Rashid said. "Our motto could be 'No mystery too big or too small.'"

"Why would we call it the Ace Detective Club?" Gavin asked. "I don't know anyone named Ace. We should call it Gavin and Sam's Detective Club, since we're the ones who started it."

Will shook his head. "I think that's a terrible idea. It makes it sound like the rest of us don't count."

"Besides, it doesn't sound very professional," Marja pointed out. "I think we should have a name that sounds professional."

"Okay, how about the Second-Grade Sleuths?" Gavin asked. "Or the Dangerous Detectives Society?"

"How about we just call it the World's Best Detective Club?" Sam said. "Our motto could be 'We're on your case.'"

"I think that's a good name," Emily

said, and everyone else nodded.

"I like it that we're the world's best," Rashid said.

"I've always wanted to be the world's best at something," Will said.

Sam liked the idea of being the world's best too. He guessed it would probably be more true to say that they were their school's best detective club, or the second grade's best detective club. But his dad always told him to set goals and dream big. Besides, if they worked hard and found lots of clues, maybe they would become the world's best detective club.

All they needed was a really good case to crack.

Chapter Five

The World's Best Bird-Lovers' Club

"So when we call ourselves the World's Best Detective Club, are we saying that we're the best detectives?" Gavin asked at their first meeting. "Or that we have the best club?"

"I think it should be both," Marja said.

"Especially since Mrs. Haynie let us use the conference room for our meetings," Emily added. "Nobody else's club gets to meet here. That means we're the best."

It turned out that Mrs. Haynie was the world's biggest bird lover if you didn't count Emily Early. She'd actually clapped her hands and jumped up and down two times when Sam asked if their bird-watching club could meet in the library.

"I adore birds!" Mrs. Haynie had told him. "I am the birdiest of bird lovers."

On the one hand, Sam thought this was good news. Their club could meet in the library conference room, which had a nice round table and a watercooler. Mrs. Haynie said they could drink all the water they wanted during their meetings if they brought their own cups.

On the other hand, Sam thought that if Mrs. Haynie discovered they were really a detective club, she'd be supermad and probably a little disappointed.

Sam liked Mrs. Haynie. He didn't want her to be mad *or* disappointed.

"I think we should spend at least five minutes every meeting talking about birds," Sam told everyone at their first meeting. "Just so Mrs. Haynie doesn't get suspicious. Also then it won't seem weird that our bird-watching club holds meetings inside instead of outside where there are actual birds."

"Good point," Emily said. "I know lots of topics we could discuss. Like why birds have beaks instead of teeth, for instance."

"Why *do* birds have beaks instead of teeth?" Rashid asked. "I never even thought about that."

"Evolution," Emily said. "They probably used to have teeth back when they were dinosaurs. But now they don't. Some people think it's because teeth were too heavy and made it hard to fly."

"So how do they chew up worms if they don't have teeth?" Gavin asked. "Do they just slurp them down like spaghetti?"

"Their digestive system grinds the worms up," Emily explained.

"So they swallow, and then they chew?" Gavin asked.

"Something like that," Emily said.

"Does this club have a president?" Will asked. "Because I think we should have a president."

Everybody looked around the table at everybody else. Sam thought Emily should probably be president. She was the smartest, plus she knew the most about birds. Still, the club had been his idea, so he felt weird about letting Emily be in charge.

Plus, this really wasn't a bird-watching club.

Sam had almost forgotten that.

"Maybe Emily and Sam should be co-presidents," Gavin suggested. "Emily could be in charge of bird information, and Sam can be in charge of detectiving."

"*Detectiving?*" Sam asked. "Is that a word?"

"I don't think it is," Gavin admitted. "But I don't know the right word to describe what we're going to be doing."

"Spying?" Rashid said.

"Sneaking?" Marja said.

"Snooping?" Will said.

"I don't know what you call it," Emily said, which Sam thought was nice. Sometimes really smart people didn't like to admit they didn't know something.

"We'll just call it being detectives," Sam decided. "That's what I'll be in charge of."

"So what's our first big case, Mr. Detective President?" Gavin asked.

Everyone looked at Sam. He took a sip of water, then cleared his throat.

"I don't know," he said. "I was hoping someone would steal something so we could find it, but so far I haven't heard about anything getting stolen."

"Hutch lost his jacket on Monday," Rashid said. "Maybe someone stole that."

"He left it on the bus," Marja said. "He always leaves his jacket on the bus, and then the next day he goes to lost and found, and it's always there."

"You can find all kinds of good stuff

at lost and found," Gavin said. "Like if you forgot your pencil? You can just go to lost and found and grab one. Mrs. Mason doesn't even ask you any questions, like, 'Are you sure that's your pencil?'"

"One time I went to look for my hat, and I saw a backpack that looked like a cat," Rashid said. "I mean, it was furry and it had a tail and everything. It wasn't real though."

"Is it still there?" Sam asked. He could feel the little spark of a plan forming in his brain.

"I saw it last year," Rashid said. "So it's probably gone now."

"They give all the leftover stuff away at the end of the year," Emily said. "To charity."

"Even the pencils?" Gavin asked.

"I guess so," Emily said. "But maybe they give the pencils to the teachers so they'll have extras when school starts again."

"I think I have our first case," Sam announced, and everyone leaned forward.

"Is it the case of the missing pencils?" Gavin asked.

"Sort of, but not really," Sam said. "I think we should go to lost and found and look for the most interesting things they've got. Then we'll see if we can find who the stuff belongs to."

"We'll be heroes!" Marja said. "I wonder if people will give us rewards."

Sam liked the idea of rewards. Getting a reward would be almost as good as getting paid to solve a case.

"A job well done is its own reward,"

Gavin said, shaking his finger at the rest of the group. "That's what Grandpop says."

"I'd rather have candy," Marja said.

"Getting a reward would be nice," Sam said. "But just solving a mystery would be nice too."

"Because solving mysteries is fun," Emily added.

"Exactly," Sam said. He looked at the clock on the wall of the conference room. "Okay, we've got seven minutes left until recess is over. Who wants to go to lost and found and get started?"

Everyone raised their hands.

"All right then," Sam said. "We've got a plan."

Chapter Six

Dog Earrings and Stuffed Snakes

The lost-and-found closet was in the main office, near Mrs. Mason's desk. Mrs. Mason was the school secretary. She was famous for wearing a different pair of dog earrings every day. Today, Sam noticed, she was wearing her Dalmation earrings. He could tell they were Dalmations from their black ears and black spots.

"I like her cocker spaniel earrings

best," Gavin whispered as they walked into the main office. "They have real fake fur on them."

"How may I help you?" Mrs. Mason said, peering at them from over her glasses. "Please don't tell me you're all sick and need to go home."

No one said anything. Sam realized as the person in charge of detecting he

should probably be the one to speak. But what should he say?

"You're not here because you're all in trouble, are you?" Mrs. Mason asked. Sam had a feeling she was kidding, but it was impossible to tell. Mrs. Mason wasn't the sort of person who used a lot of facial expressions.

Everyone looked at Sam. He guessed he better act presidential before they all got in trouble.

"We were wondering if we could look in the lost-and-found closet," he said.

"Did you lose something?" Mrs. Mason asked. "Tell me what it is and I'll tell you if it's been turned in."

"Not exactly," Sam said. "We just kind of wanted to . . ."

Sam wasn't sure how to end that sentence. How could he say what they wanted to do without letting Mrs. Mason know about their club? Everyone had agreed that keeping the World's Best Detective Club a secret was a good idea. Besides, if they said they had a detective club and wanted to solve mysteries, Mrs. Mason might say they weren't allowed to have a detective club at school without getting the principal's approval. Maybe they would have to agree to follow school rules that would make having a club no fun.

Emily stepped forward. "Our teacher, Mr. Pell, has been talking to us about being good community members," she told Mrs. Mason. "We thought we could help our fellow students by figuring out who some of the things in the lost-and-found closet belong to."

"But only the interesting lost stuff," Gavin added. "Not the pencils."

Mrs. Mason ignored Gavin and turned to Emily. "That's a very nice idea. Do you know someone who has lost something?"

"No," Emily said. "But we thought maybe we could pick a few things and try to find their owners."

"Sort of like we were solving a mystery," Sam added, thinking maybe this is what Mr. Stockfish meant by hiding in plain sight. If he pretended they were pretending to be detectives, then Mrs. Mason might never guess they really *were* detectives. "But not really like solving a mystery. I mean, that's not why we're doing this or anything."

"Shhh!" Marja shushed from behind him.

Mrs. Mason gave Sam a suspicious look. "Why don't you children pick out three items and see if you can track down their owners. If you can't find them by Friday, return the items to the closet."

The members of the World's Best Detective Club all nodded. Emily turned to Sam. "Why don't you and I pick the things?"

"Since you're the presidents and all," Gavin added.

"Shhh!" Marja shushed him.

Sam didn't know if a shusher was a good thing for a detective club to have or not. Every time Marja shushed someone it made it seem like they were keeping secrets.

On the other hand, sometimes someone really needed to tell Gavin to shush.

Sam and Emily walked over to the closet. Sam opened the door. There were approximately ten thousand things inside, most of them jackets and hoodies.

"What if there's nothing interesting?" Sam whispered to Emily.

"Don't worry," Emily whispered back. "There will be."

"If you could find the owners of some of those jackets, I'd be eternally grateful," Mrs. Mason said from her desk. "It drives me crazy when parents don't write their children's names in their jackets."

Just then the phone rang. "You kids keep it down, please," Mrs. Mason said. "This is an important call."

"We will, Mrs. Mason," Gavin said. "We promise. We're very good at keeping quiet."

"Shhh!" Marja said.

"Let's take one jacket, just to make Mrs. Mason happy," Sam whispered to Emily.

"That's a good plan, Sam," Emily whispered back, pulling out a red rain jacket with a small soccer ball patch sewn on the front. She handed it to Sam, who handed it to Will, who handed it to Marja, who handed it to Rashid, who handed it to Gavin.

"Why do I have to carry everything?" Gavin asked.

"Shhh!" Marja said.

Sam stuck his hand inside the pile of jackets and hoodies, feeling around for something more interesting. He hoped nobody had lost their pet snake. That idea made him want to pull his hand back, but he figured any lost snakes had probably slithered over to the cafeteria to get something to eat. He pushed his arm farther in and wriggled his fingers. Something poked him in the wrist. Sam grabbed it and pulled it out.

"What is it?" Will asked from behind him. "Is it something good?"

It was a black metal box with a handle. It had a lid with a clasp, and the clasp was locked with a small combination lock. Sam shook the box. Something rattled inside.

"It sounds like rocks!" Rashid said.

"Or gold!" Marja said.

"It's probably just somebody's lunch money," Emily said. "But you never know."

Sam handed the box to Marja, who handed it to Will, who handed it to Gavin.

"You pick the last thing," Sam told Emily.

"Okay," Emily said. She reached her hand into the closet. She wriggled it around and moved her arm up and down.

"There really are a lot of jackets in here," she said.

"It's a disgrace," Mrs. Mason said from her desk.

"Oh, I feel something fuzzy!" Emily exclaimed.

"I love fuzzy!" Marja said.

"Everybody loves fuzzy," Rashid said.

"I sort of like smooth stuff better," Will said.

"I can't tell what this fuzzy thing is," Emily said. She started to pull. "Maybe a stuffed elephant? I think I've got its trunk."

She pulled some more. And then she pulled even more.

"It's a snake!" she yelled after she'd pulled the whole thing out.

Sam backed away from the closet. "A snake? A real snake?"

"Not real," Emily told him. "Stuffed."

"It's a million feet long!" Marja yelled.

"Cool!" Rashid and Will yelled.

"I think I'm going to need help holding that," Gavin yelled.

"Would everyone please stop yelling?" Mrs. Mason stood up, still holding the phone to her ear. "Oh, the snake!" she said, when she saw what was in Gavin's arms. "I'd forgotten that was in there. It's been there since the second week of school. How do you lose a six-foot-long stuffed snake? That's my question."

Sam thought it was a good question.

He hoped that they were going to figure out the answer.

Chapter Seven

The Looking-for-Clues Blues

"So let me get this straight," Annabelle said after dinner that night. "You have a jacket, a box, and a snake, and you don't know who they belong to."

Sam and Annabelle were sitting on the couch watching a TV show. When Annabelle told Sam that the show was about flipping houses, he couldn't wait to see someone throw a house up into the air and make it turn upside down.

Unfortunately, Sam discovered, that's not what *flipping* meant when it came to houses. The show was actually about two guys who bought old places and fixed them up and sold them for a lot of money.

"You're not going to tell anyone, right?" Sam asked. "I mean, about our secret club?"

"Exactly who would I tell, Sam? I'm in sixth grade. Sixth graders don't care about second-grade clubs."

"That's too bad," Sam said. "They're missing out on a lot."

Annabelle shrugged. "Maybe. A detective club *does* sound interesting. So what clues do you have so far?"

"Not a lot," Sam said. "Rashid took home the metal box to see if he could figure out the combination to the lock. He likes doing puzzles and math. Once we get the box open, we'll know a lot more."

"So how about the red jacket?"

Sam shrugged. "It's a red jacket. No name tag. No label. The only thing that makes it different is that it has a soccer ball patch on the front."

"Is it a winter jacket?" Annabelle asked. "Or a rain jacket, or what?"

"Rain jacket," Sam said. "I think it's weird it doesn't have a label."

"Don't you think it's weird it doesn't have a name tag, either?"

Sam thought about this. "None of the jackets in the lost and found have name tags. Otherwise they wouldn't be lost. Also the jacket is pretty big, like it probably belongs to an older kid, maybe a fourth or fifth grader. Does Dad still write your name in your jackets?"

"Yeah, usually," Annabelle said. "Jackets are expensive. But maybe this kid's parents forgot. It happens. That still doesn't explain the missing label."

"It looks like somebody cut it out," Sam said. "And that the scissors they used weren't very good."

"Like art-room scissors?" Annabelle asked.

"Exactly!" Sam said. "Those are the worst scissors ever."

Annabelle nodded in agreement. "The art-room scissors in middle school are lots better. But if someone used art-room scissors to cut out the label, you have at least one clue."

A clue? What kind of clue did they have? Sam tried to think this through. There was a lost jacket with a missing label. There were little ragged pieces of fabric left where the label had been. Whoever had cut it out didn't have a pair of sharp scissors.

"A kid cut out the label," Sam declared. "But was it the kid who the jacket belonged to, or a kid who was pulling a prank?"

"I don't know, Sam," Annabelle said. "But here's a question for you: What if the jacket wasn't lost?"

"But it *was* lost," Sam said. "Otherwise why would it be in the lost and found?"

"Shhh!" Annabelle said, holding up her hand. "The show's back on!"

How could a jacket be in the lost and

found and not be lost? That didn't make sense to Sam. Unless, he thought, whoever it belonged to had lost it on purpose. Sam popped off the couch and ran upstairs.

Sam had stuffed the jacket in his backpack at the end of school so he could study it for clues when he got home. Now he pulled it out and rubbed his finger under the spot where the label had been. When Sam's dad put name tags in his jackets, he wrote Sam's name on a piece of special tape and stuck the tape below the jacket label. If you pulled the tape off, there was always a little bit of stickiness left.

Yep! Sam found it! There was a sticky spot in this jacket too, right underneath where the label had been.

He had found a real, live clue. There had been a name tag inside the jacket, but someone had taken it off. He went back downstairs to tell Annabelle. "I think the jacket was lost on purpose. Whoever it belonged to cut the label out and pulled the name tag off."

"But why didn't he pull off that little soccer ball thingy?"

Sam tugged at the patch on the front of the jacket. It didn't budge. "I think it would be hard to get it off. And maybe the person who was trying to lose the jacket forgot the patch was there."

"Good sleuthing, Sam the Man," Annabelle said. "Now the question is, *why*? Why did this kid lose his jacket on purpose?"

"I don't know," said Sam. "But I have a plan to find out."

"What's your plan, Sam?" Annabelle asked.

"I'm going to wear the jacket to school tomorrow," Sam said. "And then I'm going to see what happens next."

Chapter Eight

The Red Jacket Plan

"That jacket is too big for you, Sam," Gavin said the next morning on the bus. "Does your mom think you're going to grow a lot this year?"

"It's not my jacket," Sam whispered. "It's the lost-and-found jacket. I'm trying to figure out why someone would try to lose it on purpose."

"What makes you think someone tried to lose it on purpose?" Gavin whispered back.

"Because they cut out the label *and* tore off the name tag."

"So no one would know it was theirs?" Gavin asked.

"Exactly," Sam said. "But what we don't know is why."

"Maybe they hated the jacket," Gavin said. "But their parents wouldn't buy them a new one until they'd grown out of this one. So they lost it."

"But why did they hate it?" Sam asked. "That's what I'm going to try to figure out."

Emily was waiting for Sam outside of Mr. Pell's class when he and Gavin got to school. "Have you figured out any clues about the jacket yet?"

Sam told her about the missing name tag and label. "I'm trying to figure out why someone would lose this jacket on purpose. It seems like a perfectly good jacket to me."

"It's supposed to rain later," Emily said. "Maybe you'll find out that the jacket doesn't do a good job of keeping you dry."

"Or maybe the problem is that it doesn't smell very good," Gavin said, sniffing. "It didn't stink when we were on the bus, but now it's sort of starting to smell bad."

Sam sniffed too. Gavin was right. The jacket smelled like the inside of a new plastic storage box when you first took off the lid. It smelled like chemicals and a little bit like wet chickens.

"But why are we just noticing that it smells bad now?" Sam asked Emily and Gavin. "Why didn't we notice it on the bus?"

"It's hotter in school than on the bus," Gavin said.

"And you've been wearing it since you left your house this morning," Emily said. "So your body heat is warming it up too."

"But if I had a stinky jacket, I'd tell my parents I needed a new one," Sam said. "I wouldn't just toss it into the lost and found."

"Parents don't believe stuff like that though," Gavin said. "They say, 'Oh, you're just imagining that it stinks. I paid a lot of money for that jacket!'"

It's true, Sam thought. That was just the sort of thing his parents would say. "I think I'm going to take this jacket off now," he told Gavin and Emily. "I don't want to smell like a wet chicken in a plastic storage box for the rest of the day."

Sam hung the jacket up on a peg in the hallway outside the classroom. When he went into the classroom, he found a note on his desk.

Important meeting of the Bird-Watchers Club today at recess! Emily had written. *Don't miss it!*

Of course Sam wouldn't miss it. He was co-president, wasn't he? Besides, he wanted to know if anyone else had found any clues.

"Oh, here come my favorite bird-watchers!" Mrs. Haynie said when Sam and Emily and the rest of club walked into the library at recess. "What are you going to discuss today?"

"We are going to talk about vocabulary," Emily informed her. "For instance, do you

know that bird-watchers call themselves 'twitchers'?"

"I did indeed!" Mrs. Haynie exclaimed. "Oh, I wish I could sit in on your meeting, but the kindergarteners are coming in for story time."

"Maybe next time," Emily said. "We have lots more fascinating bird topics to discuss."

Sam watched as Mrs. Haynie fluttered off toward the library's story corner. Then he turned to Emily and said, "We probably shouldn't make a big deal about inviting her to our club meetings."

"It's okay," Emily replied as she led the group into the conference room. "Somebody's always coming in for story time."

"It's true," Gavin agreed, taking a seat. "We have it this afternoon at two o'clock.

Chapter seven of *The Last of the Really Great Whangdoodles!*"

"I love that book," Marja said. She sat down next to Gavin. "Magical creatures are my favorite."

"I like books about basketball better," Will said. "Or football. Or soccer. Not so much baseball, though."

"I like books about outer space," Rashid said. "But magical creatures in outer space are good too."

Emily cleared her throat. "Okay, maybe we should get started with our bird vocabulary in case anybody asks us later what we did at our club meeting. Today's first word is 'lifer.'"

"Like someone who goes to jail for their entire lives?" Gavin asked. "What does that have to do with birds?"

"No, that's a different thing," Emily said. "A lifer is a bird that you've seen for the first time in your life."

"I don't think that makes sense," Marja said. "It sounds like a bird you see all of your life. Like those little brown birds that are everywhere? Those seem more like lifer birds to me."

"It doesn't matter," Sam told Marja. "Just write it down, and then Emily can tell us another word, and then we can talk about detective stuff."

"That's right," Emily said. "So you should write down 'twitcher,' and after that write 'lifer.'"

"With an *f* or a *ph*?" Gavin asked.

"*F*," Emily said. "And the third word today is 'patch.' A patch is a place you go to look for birds."

"Like a pumpkin patch?" Rashid asked.

"I saw a crow at a pumpkin patch once," Will said. "Only it wasn't a real crow. It was made out of a black sock."

Sam looked around the table. Everyone looked confused. "I think we should just write down the words and definitions that Emily tells us," he said. "And then we can talk about my stinky jacket."

"Okay," Gavin said after he put down his pencil a minute later. "Let's talk clues."

Sam told the club about the cutout label and the sticky spot where a name tag probably had been and how the jacket started to smell weird when it got hot.

"I think the person who owns this jacket lost it on purpose," Sam finished up. "Not only did he pull off the name tag, but he cut out the label that came with the jacket."

"Which might have also had his name on it," Emily pointed out. "Some parents like to write their kids' names everywhere."

"Hutch's mom has started putting glow-in-the-dark letters that spell out *Hutch* on the back of his jackets," Marja said. "But he still keeps losing them."

Will raised his hand. "So how do you find the owner of a stinky red jacket that doesn't have any name tags or labels on it, especially if he doesn't want to be found?"

"Or she," Rashid said. "You can't even tell if that's a girl jacket or a boy jacket."

"I might be mad if someone gave me back a stinky jacket," Gavin said. "Especially one I'd lost on purpose. I mean, what if his mom already got him a new jacket? And then he brings this one home and she's all, *I can't believe I bought you a new jacket when this one was in the lost and found!*"

Sam had to admit that Gavin had a point. "Maybe we could find out who the jacket belongs to and then decide whether or not to give it back," he told the group. "I don't want to get anybody in trouble."

"Especially not over a jacket that smells bad," Emily said. "But how are we going to find out who the jacket belongs to?"

"I guess we have to wait until it rains," Sam said with a shrug. "And then we look around to see who's not wearing a jacket."

Marja pointed to the window. "It's raining right now," she said. "But everyone's out on the playground anyway."

Gavin jumped up from his seat. "Let's go!"

Everyone followed him out of the room. Mrs. Haynie looked up from the book she was reading to the kindergarteners and called, "Are you done with your meeting already?"

"Seagulls!" Sam called back. He didn't think that was a lie, since he didn't actually say they'd seen a seagull or were looking for a seagull. He'd just said the word "seagulls." Still, he felt a little weird. Sooner or later, they were going to have tell Mrs. Haynie what they were really up to at their club meetings.

But right now, it was time to find the wettest kid on the playground.

Chapter Nine

A Rainy-Day Soccer Game

At Sam's school, the teachers liked to get kids outdoors as much as possible. They liked to remind students that unless there was pouring rain, thunder and lightning, or a blizzard, recess was always outdoors.

"Put on your hats and scarves!" they'd say if it was about to snow.

"Put on your raincoats!" they'd say if it was about to rain.

Which is why when the members of the World's Greatest Detective Club reached the playground, almost everyone was wearing a jacket. It was only raining a little bit, but it was raining enough that the teachers would yell at you if you were outside without a raincoat on. Sam saw yellow jackets and blue jackets and red jackets and three camouflage jackets. He wondered if all the red jackets smelled as bad as the one from the lost and found, which he had grabbed from the peg outside of his classroom to see if it would catch anyone's attention.

And he wondered if there was some kid on the playground who *should* be wearing a stinky red rain jacket but wasn't because he'd lost it on purpose.

"Spread out, guys!" Gavin yelled. "And

report back here in five minutes!"

Sam decided to check out the soccer field first, since the kid who the jacket belonged to probably liked soccer. Sam supposed it was possible he hated soccer and that's why he (or she) tried to lose the jacket, but you'd have to hate soccer an awful lot to lose your jacket on purpose. Besides, if you hated soccer, why would someone buy you a jacket with a soccer ball patch on it in the first place?

On his way to the field, Sam thought about how being a detective made you think about stuff in a curious, question-y way. It was like PE class for your brain. For instance, his school had two playing fields, so which one should he go to? Well, he was looking for a kid big enough for this jacket to fit, so that meant he should go to the big field, the one where mostly fourth and fifth graders played. But as far as Sam could tell when he got to the sidelines, everybody on the big field was wearing a jacket, except for the goalie, who was wearing a hoodie.

"What smells?" a kid standing next to Sam asked. He looked at Sam. "Are you wearing your big brother's raincoat? Because it's about twelve sizes too big for you."

"I don't have a big brother," said Sam, puffing out his chest so the jacket wouldn't look so humongous on him.

"But you definitely have a stinky raincoat," the kid said. He moved a few feet away. "You should wash that when you get home."

Sam felt his cheeks grow hot. He wished he could explain that he was a detective on a case and that this was a lost-and-found jacket, not his own. But he didn't want to blow his cover, so he didn't say anything.

The rain was starting to come down harder. Pretty soon one of the teachers huddled by the door was going to blow a whistle and make everyone come in. The kids playing soccer kept running up and down the field, but now they were running faster, like they were trying to speed up the game so they could finish it before they had to go inside.

As the rain came down harder, Sam saw that there was one boy who wasn't wearing a jacket. He was running faster than everyone, like maybe he could run in between the raindrops. As he got closer to Sam, Sam wondered if the boy was going to run into him. If he did, Sam was pretty sure it would hurt a whole bunch. He hopped a few steps back, to be on the safe side.

"Where'd you get that jacket?" the boy yelled when he was only a few feet away. He kept running, but he kept his eyes on Sam as he went down the field.

"Do you want it?" Sam yelled back.

"No way!" The boy's face was all squinched up like he was angry. "It stinks!"

Sam turned to the boy standing next to him. "Do you know who that is?"

"Chris Gutentag," the kid answered him. "I'd watch out for him if I were you. He eats first graders for lunch."

"That's okay," Sam said. "I'm in second grade."

Still, he was happy when he heard the teacher's whistle blow.

Gavin was waiting for Sam inside the school entrance. "So did you find out who the jacket belonged to?"

Sam nodded. "I think so," he said. "This guy playing soccer gave me a funny look when he saw the jacket, and then he told me that it smelled bad. But he wasn't really close enough to know how it smelled."

"Sounds like he's probably who we're looking for," Gavin agreed. "So are you going to give it back?"

Sam and Gavin started walking down the hall toward their classroom. "I don't think he wants it back," Sam said, shivering a little as he remembered the angry expression on Chris Gutentag's face. "But I don't want to turn it back in to the lost and found. Not when we know who it belongs to. I mean, it's not really a lost jacket."

"I guess what to do with the stinky jacket is just one more mystery to solve," Gavin said. "It doesn't seem right to throw it away."

Sam thought about this. He didn't

think you should throw clothes away just because they smelled bad. Was there a way to make the jacket smell better?

"Maybe we could spray perfume on it," he told Gavin. "That might help."

"Maybe," Gavin said. "But what happens when the perfume loses its smell? Or what if perfume makes it smell even worse?"

"I guess I'll take the jacket home until we come up with a plan," Sam said. "I'll put in the garage so I don't have to smell it."

"You know what's mysterious to me?" Gavin asked as they reached their classroom. When Sam shook his head, he continued, "Besides the stinky jacket, the stuff we took from the lost and found doesn't seem like stuff that would stay lost. I mean, if I lost a six-foot-long snake, the first place I'd look for it would be the lost and found. And if I lost a box I'd put a lock on? An important box? Same thing— I'd go right to the lost and found."

Sam thought Gavin had a good point. He could see how if you lost a book or a hoodie, you might sort of forget about it, even if your parents kept reminding you to check the lost and found. But a stuffed snake? If you liked your stuffed snake enough to bring it to school, you'd go look for it the minute you realized you'd lost it.

You wouldn't lose a snake on purpose, would you?

Sam didn't think so.

"Maybe someone stole the snake from somebody's house," Sam said. "And they were hiding it in the lost and found until . . . until . . . I don't know. Until they moved or something."

"Maybe," Gavin said as they sat down at their desks. "Anyway, congratulations on solving our club's first mystery!"

"Thanks," Sam said. "I just hope our other two cases will be this easy to solve."

"I don't think they will be," Gavin said. He opened his math book. "I think this case was like two plus three, and the next two cases will be like twenty-nine minus seventeen."

Sam had a feeling Gavin was right.

Chapter Ten

The Mystery of the Six-Foot Snake

"Now why would anybody own a stuffed snake in the first place, much less bring it to school?"

Mr. Stockfish shook his head like he couldn't believe the silly things the kids at Sam's school did. "Believe you me, back in my day you didn't bring anything to school besides your books, your pencil, and your milk money. You'd get sent home if you walked through the doors carrying a snake."

Sam was pouring feed into the chicken's feeder, but he turned to look at Mr. Stockfish. "Even a stuffed snake?"

"Especially a stuffed snake!" Mr. Stockfish huffed. "At least a real snake has scientific value. But a stuffed snake? What are you supposed to do with that?"

"You could pretend it was a real snake," Sam suggested.

Mr. Stockfish shook his head. "Didn't you just tell me this snake has pink and purple and blue stripes? Does that sound like a real snake to you? Besides, if you wanted to pretend you had a real snake, you could get a rubber snake. I could understand a rubber snake."

Sam guessed Mr. Stockfish was right. But he could also understand why you might want a six-foot-long stuffed snake with pink and purple and blue stripes, even if it wasn't practical or scientific.

"What I don't get is how do you lose a snake like that?" Sam asked as he put the lid back on the feed bin. "It's not like a button or even a basketball. It's not something you could drop without noticing that you dropped it. It couldn't roll away on its own."

"Well, if you didn't lose it, then somebody had to take it," Mr. Stockfish said. "Only it would be a hard thing to steal if anyone else was around. You can't just slip a six-foot snake under your notebook."

"You'd have to take it when no one was looking," Sam agreed. "But if the snake was stolen, how did it end up in the lost and found? And why didn't its owner go look for it there?"

Mr. Stockfish picked up his chicken, Leroy, and patted her on the head. "That's your mystery right there, Sam. Why has no one claimed that snake?"

"But how do I solve the mystery?" Sam asked.

"That's why you have a club, isn't it?" Mr. Stockfish asked. "You all need to put your brains together. But let me make one suggestion: if you want to know what's really going on in a school, there's one person you should ask."

"The principal?"

"The janitor," Mr. Stockfish said. "My uncle Roy in Chicago was a janitor, and he knew everything that happened in the school where he worked. He knew things nobody else knew."

The janitor at Sam's school was named

Mr. Truman. Sometimes Sam saw him in Miss Fran's art classroom when she wasn't teaching anyone. Mr. Truman was famous at their school for his paintings of trees.

Was it possible he had information about the stuffed snake? Why not, Sam thought? Mr. Truman was in and out of classrooms all day, cleaning up spills, replacing lightbulbs, and emptying out trash cans. Sam bet a six-foot-long snake would have caught his attention.

"Talking to the janitor sounds like a good plan," he told Mr. Stockfish. "I'll look for him when I get to school tomorrow."

"Take the members of your club with you," Mr. Stockfish advised Sam. "Six heads are better than one."

◉ ◉ ◉

The members of the World's Best Detective Club met outside Mr. Truman's office as soon as their buses dropped them off at school the next morning. Sam had called Gavin the night before to tell him about Mr. Stockfish's idea, and then Gavin called everyone else to tell them to meet.

"I think that officially makes me the club's communications director," Gavin said. "That's what my mom told me. She said I could put it on my résumé."

"What's a résumé?" Marja asked.

"It's a piece of paper where you make a list of all the good stuff you've done so you can get a job," Gavin told her. "I started writing mine last night. So far I've got 'cleaned my room the day before school started' and 'remembered to put my used Kleenex in the trash two weeks ago.' Oh, and I put that I'm communications director for our club, which means I'm the person who calls everyone."

"I got a kitten out of a tree once," Rashid said. "Could I put that on my résumé?"

"I think so," Gavin said. "It would be especially good if you wanted a job as a tree climber."

"Or a cat saver," Will said.

"I like dogs better than cats," Marja said.

"So you would have just left that cat up the tree?" Gavin asked.

Marja thought about this. "I guess not," she said after a moment. "But if there was a dog up the same tree, I'd save it first."

Mr. Truman poked his head out of his door. "I thought I heard somebody out here. Do you guys need something, or is this just where you decided to hang out this morning?"

"Do you have time to answer a few questions about a snake?" Sam asked.

"A snake?" Mr. Truman looked alarmed.

"Not a real snake!" Sam added quickly. "A stuffed snake."

"About six feet long?" Gavin added.

"With purple and pink and blue stripes?" Emily said.

"Come in," Mr. Truman said, waving the children into his office. "The snake you're describing sounds familiar."

"Did you know it was in the lost and found?" Sam asked as he followed Mr. Truman inside. "It was buried under a ton of jackets."

"I think this school has set the record for lost jackets," Mr. Truman said. "I find at least six in the cafeteria every day. Most of them have name tags inside, but there's always one that doesn't. So the snake was in the lost and found?"

"Mrs. Mason said it's been in there since the second week of school," Emily informed him.

"That's a clue!" Gavin said, sounding like he'd just realized this.

"Shhh!" Marja said.

Mr. Truman took a seat behind his desk. "Here's what I can tell you about that snake," he said, leaning back with his hands clasped behind his head. "It showed up in Mrs. Ybarra's classroom on the first day of school. I noticed it when I was emptying trash cans at the end of the day. It was pushed against the wall, but it was near a row of desks, like it belonged to somebody, but that student had been asked to put it a little bit out of the way. Sometimes when I went in during the school day, the snake wasn't there, and once I went in during lunch and the snake was curled up over in the reading nook. But at the end of the day, it was always back in the same place, against the wall, near the desks."

"When did you notice it was wasn't there anymore?" Rashid asked.

"The following Monday," Mr. Truman said. "I went in to empty the trash cans after school was over, and the snake was gone. I thought that its owner must have finally taken it home."

"What grade does Mrs. Ybarra teach?" Emily asked.

"Fourth grade. She's in room 125, near

the gym." Mr. Truman smiled. "I like Mrs. Ybarra. She keeps a very neat classroom. You go in the room at the end of the day and all the desks are in straight lines, no trash on the floor. She makes my life easy."

"So it sounds like the lost-and-found

snake belongs to someone in Mrs. Ybarra's class," Sam said to the other club members. "All we have to do is bring it back to her classroom and see who wants it."

"I'll bring it to school tomorrow," Emily said. "We can take it at recess."

"That sounds like a good plan," said Sam. He turned to Mr. Truman. "By the way, you don't know anything about how to make a rain jacket less stinky, do you?"

"Try washing it with a solution of vinegar and baking soda, and then air it out to dry," Mr. Truman said.

Sam didn't know you could wash rain jackets, but he guessed it made sense. After all, they were made to get wet. "Thanks," he told Mr. Truman. "And thanks for telling us where the snake came from."

"Be sure to let me know if you find its

owner," Mr. Truman said as he stood up. "You don't see a snake like that every day."

"You really don't," Sam agreed. Which was probably a good thing, he thought. Who could get any work done with a striped snake by your desk? A chicken, maybe, but a snake?

Maybe that's why the snake had been put in the lost and found—no one could learn anything while it was around.

Sam hoped they were about to find out.

Chapter Eleven

The Disappearing Fake Snake

It was sort of weird to walk down the hall carrying a six-foot-long snake, Sam thought the next day at recess, even one that was in a big plastic trash bag. A lot of kids stared, and a few yelled out guesses about what was in the bag. One person guessed it was a teacher's dirty laundry, and another person guessed it was the world's biggest bag of popcorn.

"It's a snake!" Gavin said when someone guessed that they were lugging a misbehaving kindergartner to the principal's office. "Can't anyone recognize a snake in a bag when they see one?"

That made a bunch of people yell and start running.

Gavin shook his head. "I mean, it's perfectly obvious that's what it is, right?"

Sam hoped they would reach Mrs. Ybarra's room before they got arrested for bringing snakes to school.

"Did you try washing the jacket last night?" Emily asked Sam as they neared room 125.

"Yeah, I poured a bunch of vinegar on a sponge and scrubbed the jacket as hard as I could," Sam told her. "Now it smells worse than it did before."

"That's too bad," Emily said. "So what

are you going to try now?"

Sam shrugged. "I hung the jacket on a hook in the garage to let it air out. Maybe it will smell better after a few days."

Even though it was recess, there were a bunch of kids inside Mrs. Ybarra's classroom. One of them was working on a computer in the back, and four more were watching the computer boy. A few other people were sitting at their desks. Mrs. Ybarra was there too, and when she saw the members of the World's Greatest Detective Club standing at her doorway, she waved them inside.

"Are you guys collecting recycling for Mr. Truman?" she called from her desk. "He told me he had some student volunteers today."

Sam stepped forward. "No, we've come

to ask you a question about a snake."

"This snake in particular," Gavin said, coming up next to Sam and dumping the snake out in front of Mrs. Ybarra's chair. "Do you know anything about it?"

When Mrs. Ybarra saw the snake, she stood up. "Please take that snake out of my classroom right now. I can't have it in here."

One of the students who had been reading a book at her desk looked up. "Slimey! Look, everybody! They brought Slimey back!"

A few of the other kids yelled, "Slimey! You found Slimey!"

And two of them screamed. "No! Not Slimey!"

The first girl got up from her desk and walked to the front of the room. "Nobody

knew what happened to him," she said, leaning down to pet the snake on the head. "He just disappeared one day."

"He was sort of like our class mascot," the kid sitting at the computer said. "Only some people didn't like him very much." He pointed over to the screaming kids. "Like Charlotte and Daniel. Jackson didn't like him, either, but he's not here."

"Why was the snake—Slimey—in your class in the first place?" Rashid asked. "Were you studying reptiles? Was he supposed to be educational?"

"Kervin Mack's mom sent Slimey to school the very first day," the girl petting Slimey said. "She thought maybe Mrs. Ybarra would like a snake for the reading corner—you know, for a pillow."

"A snake pillow," Gavin said. "Interesting idea."

"It was a terrible idea," the girl named Charlotte said. "Snakes give me nightmares."

"They give me the creeps too," the boy named Daniel said. "Even stuffed snakes with pink and purple and blue stripes. What if there's an actual, real snake that looks like that? It makes me want to live on Mars."

"There could be snakes on Mars too," Will pointed out.

"Mars doesn't have the ecosystem for snakes," Daniel said. "It's a totally safe space, snake-wise."

Mrs. Ybarra walked over and took Slimey from the girl who was petting him. "I'm afraid this snake is no longer welcome here. If you would be so kind to take him back to the—I mean, just take him back. To wherever you found him."

"Were you about to say the lost and found?" Marja asked, taking notes on a small notepad.

"If that's where you found him," Mrs. Ybarra said with a shrug.

The members of the World's Best Detective Club looked at one another.

"I'm just curious," Emily said to Mrs. Ybarra. "If there were kids in your class who didn't like snakes, why didn't Kervin just take Slimey back home?"

"Kervin's mom hates that snake," the computer boy said. "She wouldn't let Kervin bring Slimey home."

"We had a lot of fights about it," Charlotte added. "It's like all we did the first week of school was fight about whether Kervin should take Slimey back home, even if his mom didn't like it. And then Slimey disappeared."

"Who's fault is that?" the computer boy asked. "A lot of people blame you, Charlotte."

"I didn't have anything to do with it," Charlotte said. "But I'm glad it happened."

Mrs. Ybarra put Slimey back in the bag and handed the bag to Gavin. "Okay, kids, recess is almost over. Why don't you take Slimey back to the lost and found?"

"But we never actually said for sure that we found Slimey at the lost—"

Mrs. Ybarra cut Gavin off. "Go on now! You're going to be late!"

The members of the World's Best Detective Club walked out of the classroom and into the hallway.

"Are you thinking what I'm thinking?" Marja asked as they started back to Mr. Pell's classroom.

"That Mrs. Ybarra put Slimey in the lost and found?" Emily asked.

"That's what I think," said Will.

"Having three people in her class who hate snakes meant that keeping a snake—even a fake snake—caused a lot of problems," Rashid said. "I can see why she wouldn't want him there."

"And if Kervin Mack's mom wouldn't take Slimey back, Mrs. Ybarra was sort of stuck," Sam said. "She couldn't just throw Slimey away. I mean, he's a pretty cool snake."

"So what are we supposed to do with Slimey now?" Emily asked. "Put him back in the lost and found? That's no fun, even if I'm pretty sure we solved the case."

Sam sighed. "Hand me the bag, Gavin. I'll store Slimey in the garage along with Chris Gutentag's rain jacket."

"Pretty soon the whole lost and found is going to be in your garage," Gavin said. "I don't think your parents are going to be too happy about that."

Sam knew that Gavin was right, but he didn't want to just give up and take everything back.

Besides, if they never made any money solving cases, he could always have a garage sale.

Chapter Twelve

T. rex Chickens

"So what are you learning in your bird-watching club?" Mr. Stockfish asked on Sunday as they walked to Mrs. Kerner's house to feed their chickens.

"At the meeting the other day, Emily told us that birds have hollow bones," Sam said. "And that chickens used to be dinosaurs."

"I wonder if she meant that chickens were *descended* from dinosaurs," Mr. Stockfish said.

"Yeah, I think that's it," Sam said. "A long time ago there were Tyrannosaurus rex dinosaurs and now there are chickens. I don't really understand how that works though."

"It takes millions of years and a lot of slow changes over time," Mr. Stockfish said. "It's interesting how different species have changed and adapted over the millennia."

"Do you think humans will ever turn into chickens?" Sam asked. "It would be neat if we could lay eggs."

"I don't think it's very likely," Mr. Stockfish said, bending over to pick up a piece of bark from the sidewalk. "This bark is shaped a little bit like a dinosaur—a *Psittacosaurus*, I'd say."

"Maybe chickens will turn back into

dinosaurs," Sam said. "That would be so cool!"

Mr. Stockfish scratched his head. "I think that could cause some problems, Sam."

"Yeah," Sam agreed. "We'd have to build a bigger coop in Mrs. Kerner's backyard for one thing. Like a *humongous* coop."

When they reached Mrs. Kerner's back gate, Sam could hear the chickens pecking and squawking. "Just imagine if they were a whole bunch of T. rexes," he said. "I still think that would be really neat."

"I think we'd be in a whole lot of trouble," Mr. Stockfish said. "What if one of them stepped on us?"

"I think we'd get stomped," Sam admitted. "I guess it's better that chickens are still birds. Did you know that owls eat their prey in one bite? It's a good thing they don't eat people. I'd hate to get eaten in one bite!"

"Me too, Sam," Mr. Stockfish said, following Sam into the backyard. "For that matter, I'd hate to get eaten in two bites."

"Or ten bites," Sam agreed.

Come to think of it, even a hundred bites would be bad, Sam thought. There was really no number of bites that would make Sam happy to be eaten by a chicken.

Sam was hungry when he got home, so he walked into the kitchen to get a frozen waffle. His mom was sitting at the table working on her laptop.

"Why is there a red jacket hanging in the garage?" she asked. "It smells terrible.

Like vinegar and that weird way plastic things smell when they're new."

"It's just some raincoat I found," Sam said. "I thought I'd try to make it smell better before I gave it back. But it turns out vinegar doesn't actually make stuff smell better."

"It does if you put it in the washer with soap and a little baking soda," his mom said.

"Can we try that?" Sam asked, grabbing a waffle out of the freezer.

"Sure, we'll run it through the wash after dinner," Sam's mom said. "But where did you find it, and why didn't you just drop it in the lost and found?"

Sam didn't know if he should tell his mom about the detective club or not. She might get excited about Sam being in a club and start making suggestions for fun things Sam's club could do. Also, she'd ask him every night at dinner, "So what did your club do today?"

He thought maybe it would be better to tell his mom about the club later, like in a few years. For now, he thought it would be okay to just tell her the sort-of truth. "Some of my friends and I are trying to find who all the lost-and-found stuff belongs to, including the stinky jackets."

"That's a great idea," Sam's mom said. "Well, you and I will do what we can to make this particular jacket less stinky." She turned back to her laptop and started to type something, then stopped. "Oh, I almost forgot. Rashid called and wants you to call him back. I wrote his phone number on the pad by the phone."

Sam almost never got calls from anyone but Gavin. He felt important all of the sudden, like the president of a big company. "Can I take the phone up to my room to call Rashid?"

"Just remember to bring it back downstairs," Sam's mom said.

Sam grabbed the phone and the phone number. As soon as he got upstairs, he sat on his bed and called Rashid.

"Do you have some news?" he asked when Rashid answered.

"I did it, Sam!" Rashid whooped. "I cracked the code!"

Sam was confused. "The code?"

"The combination! For the lock on the little black box. I did it on try number 279. And you'll never guess what I found inside!"

"What did you find?" Sam asked. "Was it something good?"

"I found another box! And guess what was inside that box?"

"What?"

Rashid laughed. "I'm not telling—not until our club meeting tomorrow. But I think it's going to make us rich."

Chapter Thirteen

The Mystery of the Box Inside the Box

"What are you going to buy after we split the money?" Gavin asked Sam on the bus the next morning. "I was thinking about getting a puppy."

"You can get a puppy for free from the animal shelter," Sam pointed out. "You don't have to be rich."

"I know, but then I'm going to build my puppy a puppy mansion in the backyard. I'll put a TV in it, and a little refrigerator."

"Why does a puppy need a TV and a refrigerator?" Sam asked.

"Oh, that's for me," Gavin explained. "I'm going to live in the puppy mansion too."

"I wonder why Rashid said that what's inside the box will make us rich," Sam said. "Isn't our job to find out who it belongs to and give it back?"

Gavin shrugged. "Maybe they don't want it anymore. Nobody else has wanted their stuff back."

"I guess we'll just have to see what it is," Sam said. "It might not even be valuable."

"Why would Rashid be so excited then?"

Sam had to admit that was a good question. If the box held an old pencil eraser or a marble collection, Rashid would have said so. That wasn't the sort of information you kept to yourself. It was too boring to make a good secret.

"Maybe it's somebody's gold wedding rings," Gavin said as the bus pulled up to school. "Remember how something rattled inside when we shook the box? Maybe one of the rings has a diamond in it!"

"Maybe," Sam said.

Gavin grinned. "I bet if it's rings, we'll get a big reward. A million bucks at least!"

A million bucks seemed like a lot to Sam, but maybe Gavin was right that they were about to get a big reward. Maybe it would be enough to buy a monster truck!

Sam would look supercool driving around town in a monster truck.

By the time Sam and Gavin got to their

classroom, school was about to start.

"I guess we're just going to have to wait until recess to find out how rich we are," Gavin said as they sat down at their desks.

"I don't know if I can wait two hours," Sam said. "I wish Rashid would just tell us now."

It took forever to get to recess. First they had to do math, then they had to do science. Math was subtraction, which Sam didn't like, but they were doing weather in science, which was neat because it meant they got to go outside a lot to study clouds. Right before recess, they had writing time. In second grade, you had to write a whole book, and when everyone was done, they would read their books to the kindergarteners. Sam's book was about a boy who ate so many frozen waffles that he turned into a frozen waffle. Usually he liked working on it, but today he was too excited about what was inside the box to focus on his story.

Finally it was time for recess. The members of the World's Greatest Detective Club asked for permission to go to the library. Sam wondered if after today they would make Rashid club president because he'd figured out how to open the box and make them all rich.

"So is it wedding rings with diamonds in them?" Gavin asked as soon as they all sat down at the conference room table. "Are they worth a million bucks?"

Rashid shook his head. "Not even close. Any other guesses?"

"I think it's gold coins," Marja said. "Like pirate treasure or something."

"Where would somebody find pirate treasure around here?" Will asked. "Forget the fact that there's no such thing as pirates."

"Actually, there were pirates," Emily said. "Edward Teach was a famous pirate known as Blackbeard. He was a real person."

"Why are we talking about pirates?" Sam asked. "I want to know what's inside the box."

"Yeah," Gavin said. "Open it!"

"Open it!" everyone else said.

"Hold your horses," Rashid said. "First I need to do the combination."

"You locked it back up?" Sam said.

"Of course I locked it back up," Rashid said. "I didn't want the treasure to get stolen!"

"He said 'treasure'!" Marja said. "See, I told you it was treasure!"

"You said it was pirate treasure," Will pointed out. "That's different from just regular treasure."

"Could you guys be quiet, please?" Rashid said. "I'm trying to remember the combination."

Everybody groaned. This is taking a century, Sam thought. He glanced nervously toward the door. Mrs. Haynie didn't have a story time group this morning. What if she walked in while Rashid was trying to remember the combination? What would they say? That there was a bird in the box? Who kept a bird in a locked box? Mrs. Haynie would never believe that.

"May I have everyone's attention, please!" Rashid said after a few more very long moments. "The lock is now off! Any other guesses about what's inside?"

"Could you just show us?" Sam asked. "My stomach is starting to hurt."

"Mine too," Will said. "This is making me nervous."

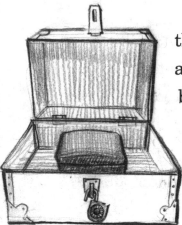

Rashid carefully lifted the box's lid. He pulled out a smaller box. It was navy blue and had a lid on it.

"See, it's a jewelry box, just like I said!" Gavin whispered excitedly to Sam.

"But it's more like the box my dad gave my mom for her birthday," Sam said. "It had a bracelet inside it, not a ring. That box is a bracelet-sized box."

"Shhh!" Marja shushed them. "Let Rashid talk!"

"There are actually three things inside this box," Rashid said as he took off the lid. "Two are the same and one is different."

"Two apples and an orange!" Gavin shouted.

"Shhh!" everyone told him.

"Here are the two things that are the same," Rashid said. He lifted two silver coins from the box. "They are John F. Kennedy half dollars."

"Are they worth a million bucks?" Gavin asked.

"No," Rashid said. "My dad helped me look it up. These were made in 1966 and are in good condition, so they're probably worth ten dollars apiece."

"Do you think twenty dollars makes us rich?" Will asked. "Because my grandma gave me twenty dollars for my birthday, and I'm pretty sure I'm not rich yet."

Rashid held up his hand. "I haven't gotten to the good part." He pulled a card out of the box. "This is what's going to make us rich. It's a Michael Jordan card from his rookie year."

"Who's Michael Jordan?" Marja asked. "And what's a rookie year?"

"A rookie year is the first year an athlete plays professionally," Rashid explained.

Mrs. Haynie stood at the door. "And Michael Jordan is one of the world's greatest basketball players," she continued. "But I'm not sure what he has to do with birdwatching."

"Mrs. Haynie, we can explain!" Emily said. "Can't we, Sam?"

"We can?" Sam asked.

Mrs. Haynie folded her arms across her chest. "I certainly hope so, Sam."

Chapter Fourteen

Sam the Man and the Explanation Plan

"I 'm waiting," Mrs. Haynie said.

Sam tried to think of something to say. Sometimes basketball players looked like they were flying, so they were sort of like birds, right? Last week in science, Emily did a report on bird flight patterns and how they were affected by the weather. Did basketball players have flight patterns? Could Sam make up something about basketball player flight patterns? Or how basketball players were affected by the weather?

He was starting to feel confused.

Maybe he should just tell the truth.

"I'm pretty sure that Michael Jordan doesn't have anything to do with bird-watching," Sam told Mrs. Haynie.

Mrs Haynie raised one eyebrow. She looked suspicious. "How about your club?"

"It doesn't have a lot to do with bird-watching either," Sam admitted. "Maybe a little bit, but not a lot."

Up until now, Mrs. Haynie had looked mad. But suddenly she just looked sad. She sank into the chair next to Gavin and said, "So you guys were lying to me? You're not really interested in birds?"

Emily stood up. "I'm very interested in birds," she said. "My life list is sixty-seven birds long. And I've been telling our club interesting bird information. I think everybody here is at least a little interested in birds."

The members of the World's Greatest Detective Club all nodded their heads, and Sam thought Mrs. Haynie looked a little less sad.

"Did you know that birds swallow, and then chew?" Gavin asked Mrs. Haynie. "That's one fascinating bird fact I've learned in this club."

"That's a good fact," Mrs. Haynie agreed, brightning a little bit. "Do you know that some birds swallow tiny pebbles to help them digest their food?"

"That's interesting," Sam said. "See, we really are learning about birds in our club."

Mrs. Haynie frowned. "But it's not really a bird-watching club. So what kind of club is it?"

Sam looked at Gavin, who looked at Emily, who looked at Will, who looked at Rashid, who looked at Marja, who looked at Sam. Sam looked at Mrs. Haynie. "It's a detective club," he told her. "We were trying to keep it a secret, in case we had top secret clues that nobody else could know. But maybe we should have told you."

"Because you're someone we could trust," said Emily. "Most bird-watchers are very trustworthy."

"I'm going to check out seven books about birds today," Gavin said. "Just to make it up to you."

"Thank you, Gavin," Mrs. Haynie said. "I appreciate that. And I wish you really would start a bird-watching club. I think other students might be interested in it too."

"Really?" Emily's eyes grew wide. "That would be awesome!"

Mrs. Haynie pointed to the silver half dollars. "So is this one of your mysteries?"

Rashid nodded. "We found a locked box in the lost and found. I figured out the combination number. Those coins and that basketball card were inside."

Mrs. Haynie leaned over so she could see the half dollars and the card better. "You found the Michael Jordan rookie card?" She blinked a few times. "When? Where?"

"Do you know who it belongs to?" Sam asked.

"Yes, it belongs to—" Mrs. Haynie

began, but then she stopped herself. "Hmmm. If you're a detective club, then maybe you should investigate for yourself. I can tell you that it was lost two weeks ago, and the person who lost it is very upset. I'm curious though—I know that this person checked the lost and found, but didn't find the box there. When did you find it?"

"Last week," Emily told her. "So maybe the box had been turned in to the lost and found after the person looked for it."

"But why didn't Mrs. Mason give it to the person it belonged to?" Will asked. "She must have known the person was looking for it."

"That's a good question!" Mrs. Haynie said. "What do you guys think?"

Everyone was quiet. "Maybe the person

who turned it in didn't give it to Mrs. Mason?" Sam said after a moment. "Maybe they just stuffed it into the lost-and-found closet when nobody was looking."

"It's a really messy closet," Gavin told Mrs. Haynie. "You could shove something in there and it would be lost forever."

Mrs. Haynie smiled. "You guys are good detectives! I'll tell you what. I'll give you the rest of the day to solve the mystery of who the box belongs to. If you solve it, you can give the box back and collect the reward. If you don't solve it, I'll give the box back and use the reward money to buy some more bird books for the library."

"Just until the end of the day?" Marja asked. "That's not enough time!"

"I'm sorry," Mrs. Haynie said. "But the person these items belong to has been very upset—not to mention in a lot of trouble for bringing the box to school to begin with. He needs to have it returned as soon as possible."

"Did you just say 'he'?" Gavin asked.

"Did I?" Mrs. Haynie said. "I don't think so."

"You did!" Rashid said. "So there's our first clue. And I bet he's in a lot of trouble for losing that card. It's worth a thousand dollars!"

A thousand dollars! Sam looked around at the other members of the World's Greatest Detective Club. Everyone's mouths had dropped wide open.

A thousand dollars!

"It would be worth even more, except one of the corners is bent," Rashid explained. "Still, that's a lot of money.

How much is the reward, Mrs. Haynie?"

"Fifty dollars," Mrs. Haynie said. "Not bad, huh?"

Sam wondered what fifty divided by six was.

One of these days he was really going to have to learn how to divide things.

"Can you give us one more clue?" Sam asked Mrs. Haynie. "This school has four hundred students. If half of them are boys, that means . . . well, that there are a lot of boys."

Mrs. Haynie seemed to give this some thought. "I'll tell you what. I'll give you one more clue if you promise to start a bird-watching club that's open to other students. I'll be your sponsor. Maybe we could even take a bird-watching field trip one day."

"We'll definitely start a club," Emily said, jumping up and down. "I bet we could get fifty people to join!"

"Or at least ten!" Marja said.

"Maybe three," Will said. "But that would still be good."

Sam looked at Mrs. Haynie. "It's a deal. So what's the clue?"

"It's very simple, Sam. If you can figure out what two half dollars and one sports card have in common, you'll figure out who they belong to."

"I don't get it," Will said.

"I know a lot about clues," Gavin said. "And that's not a very good clue."

"Think about it," Mrs. Haynie said. She glanced up at the clock on the wall. "You have until three o'clock. Good luck!"

Chapter Fifteen

The Case of the Terrible Clue

After recess Sam's class had social studies. In social studies they were studying maps, and today they were coloring maps. That meant Sam had time to think while he was coloring.

What do two half dollars and a basketball card have in common? Not much that he could tell. In the case they were trying to solve, the half dollars were worth ten dollars each, and the card was worth one thousand dollars. Sam guessed you could say that what these things sort of had in common was that they were valuable. So maybe the person the things belonged to had a lot of money?

The problem was Sam didn't know any rich people at his school. Besides, if you were rich, wouldn't you just buy new coins and a new card?

Sam wished Annabelle was sitting next to him. Her sixth-grade brain was a lot smarter than his second-grade brain. Not only could she do division, she was good at crossword puzzles and jigsaw puzzles. Mostly she was just good at figuring things out.

And if Mr. Stockfish were sitting next to Annabelle? They'd have this mystery solved in ten seconds!

Sam sighed. How was he ever going to solve the puzzle of what silver half dollars and sports cards had in common? It was impossible.

After social studies Mr. Pell's class went to PE, which gave the members of the World's Greatest Detective Club a chance to talk.

"Anyone come up with anything yet?" Emily asked as their PE teacher, Miss Chambers, pulled stuff from the equipment room. "I don't have a clue."

"Well, technically speaking, you do have a clue," Gavin told her. "It's just not a very good clue."

"Maybe it's a great clue," Rashid said. "We won't know until we solve the mystery."

"*If* we solve the mystery," Marja said. She didn't sound very confident.

"I could really use that fifty dollars," Gavin said. "I'm thinking about buying a pair of binoculars like Marja's. You know, for bird-watching."

"If we get the reward, we have to divide it up," Will pointed out. "So you wouldn't actually get the whole fifty dollars."

"Does anyone know what fifty dollars divided by six is?" Sam asked.

"Eight dollars and thirty-three cents," Rashid told him.

"Wow, you figured that out fast!" Sam said.

Rashid pointed to his head. "My dad says I've got a brain like a calculator. That's why it only took me 279 tries to figure out the combination on the lock."

Miss Chambers blew her whistle, so they had to stop talking. Today they were learning how to dribble basket-balls around orange cones. Sam thought he might like to have some orange cones for his backyard. He wasn't sure what for though. He just liked the way they looked, like rubbery orange hats.

The class spent the next thirty minutes dribbling. Every time Sam passed another member of the World's Greatest Detective Club, they shrugged their shoulders at each other. It was like they were saying, *I still haven't figured out what that stuff has in common; have you?*

"Coins and cards, coins and cards," Sam repeated to himself a hundred times as he dribbled. Metal and paper. Both of them had pictures of famous people on them. Maybe the person they belonged to collected pictures of famous people.

Or maybe the person they belonged to collected coins and cards.

Sam stopped dribbling. He stopped moving.

He knew what the coins and the cards had in common.

They were both things people collected.

Sam knew a lot of people who collected sports cards, and he knew some people were coin collectors too. But it would take days to talk to all the card and coin collectors at their school. So whoever owned the half dollars and the Michael Jordan card probably collected other things. He was probably famous for all his collections, which is why Mrs. Haynie believed they could find him by three o'clock if they figured out the clue.

Miss Chambers blew her whistle. "Sam Graham! You're holding up traffic. Get moving, mister!"

Sam started dribbling his ball again. That had to be it, right? All they had to figure out now was who to ask about the school's most famous collectors. Not every teacher knew every kid, so it would waste a lot of time to go from classroom to classroom to see if this teacher or that one had the information they needed. They needed to find somebody who would know a lot about everything.

Sam knew exactly who to ask.

The members of the World's Greatest Detective Club ate their lunches as fast as they could. Instead of going outside after they were done, however, they had a special club meeting. But instead of going to the library, they made their way down the hall to Mr. Truman's office.

"What if he's not there?" Marja asked. "Do you think it would be okay to wait?"

"If he's not there, we could just go ask Mrs. Mason," Gavin pointed out. "She knows who the box belongs to."

"How could she, if the box was put in the lost and found without her knowing about it?" Will asked as they reached Mr. Truman's office.

"I bet whoever the box belongs to asked Mrs. Mason if she'd seen it," Gavin said. "She probably helped him search the lost and found."

"But wouldn't it be cheating to ask Mrs. Mason?" Emily asked. "There's a difference between figuring something out and someone giving you the answer. I want to figure it out."

"We'd still be figuring it out," Gavin said. "We'd just be figuring it out faster."

"I guess so," Emily said. "Okay, if Mr. Truman isn't here, we'll ask Mrs. Mason."

Just then Mr. Truman's door opened and the janitor stuck his head out. "You guys sure like hanging out outside of my office," he said. "Or do you have another question for me?"

"We have another question for you," Sam said. "About another thing we found in the lost and found."

"Let me guess," Mr. Truman said, stroking his chin. "You're here to ask about the sheriff's badge I found in the gym last week. I'm surprised no one's claimed that yet. It looked real."

"Somebody lost a sheriff's badge?" Gavin asked. "That's so cool!"

"But it's not what we're here to ask about," Emily said. "Have you heard of anyone losing a box with a combination lock on it?"

Mr. Truman raised an eyebrow. "I have indeed. That box contained some very valuable property."

"That's right! Do you know who it belongs to?" Sam asked.

"I know exactly who it belongs to," Mr. Truman said. "Do you have it?"

Rashid stepped forward and held up the box so Mr. Truman could see it. Mr. Truman's eyes narrowed. "We tore through the lost-and-found closet looking for that thing," he said. "There's no way we wouldn't have seen it. So why don't you tell me how you really found the box?"

"That's how we really found it!" Gavin insisted. "You could ask—well, you could ask any person in this group!"

"You could ask Mrs. Mason," Emily said. "She was there when we found it."

"But she was on the phone," Sam said. "Remember? She wasn't paying attention when I pulled out the box. Otherwise she would have asked for it so she could give it back to whoever it belongs to."

"Guys, I hate to say this," Mr. Truman said, "but unless you can prove to me that you found this box in the lost and found, I have to wonder if you had something to do with its disappearance in the first place."

"That doesn't make sense," Sam said. "If we stole it, why would we ask you who it belongs to?"

Mr. Truman thought about this. "That's a good point, Sam. But still, it seems like something fishy is going on here."

If Sam's stomach had been hurting during recess, it was hurting even more now. Did Mr. Truman really think they were thieves? That was crazy! How could they prove they'd found the locked box in the lost and found?

Now Sam wished that they'd told everyone in the world about their club and what they were doing. Then they would have all sorts of people who could back up their story. But because they'd kept it a secret, hardly anyone knew what they were up to. Annabelle did, but who was going to believe his sixth-grade sister? They'd say she was just trying to get Sam out of trouble.

There was only one thing he could do, Sam decided. He turned to Mr. Truman. "Could I use your phone, please? There's someone very important I need to call."

Chapter Sixteen

The World's Best Detective and Bird-Watching Club

S am thought it was pretty lucky that Mr. Stockfish's daughter, Judy, had made Sam memorize their phone number in case anything happened when he and Mr. Stockfish took their walks. His fingers trembled as he punched the numbers on Mr. Truman's phone—what if he'd remembered wrong? But Mr. Stockfish picked up on the second ring.

"What do you want?" he said in a

gruff voice. "I'm watching the news."

"Is that how you always answer the phone?" Sam asked. "It's not very polite."

"Is that you, Sam Graham?" Mr. Stockfish asked. "Why aren't you at school?"

"I *am* at school," Sam told him. "And I need you to talk to the janitor."

"Did you throw up?"

"No!" Sam said. "But even if I did throw up, why would I ask you to talk to the janitor?"

"Beats me, Sam," Mr. Stockfish said. "It's just the first thing that came to mind."

That's when Sam explained that Mr. Truman didn't believe that Sam and the other members of the World's Best Detective Club had found the locked box in the lost and found.

"Well, I wasn't there when you found

it," Mr. Stockfish said when Sam was done explaining. "But I remember that you told me about it that afternoon."

Sam handed the phone to Mr. Truman. "This is a witness. Sort of."

Mr. Truman took the phone from Sam and listened. And listened. And listened some more.

It turned out Mr. Stockfish had a lot to say.

After he finally got off the phone, Mr. Truman turned to Sam and said, "Your friend has convinced me. He told me all about your club and how you're looking for the owners of things you've pulled out of the lost and found. But why didn't you tell me that in the first place?"

Sam shrugged. "I didn't think you'd believe me."

"I'm sorry, Sam," Mr. Truman said. He looked at everyone. "I apologize to all of you. When I couldn't find Aidan's box anywhere two weeks ago, his father was very angry at me. He even suggested I might have found it and kept it myself. It's been a very stressful situation."

"Aidan?" Rashid asked. "Is that who the box belongs to?"

"Yes," Mr. Truman said. "Aidan Howzer. He's a nice kid, but he's always losing stuff. He collects a lot of different things—sports cards and coins, of course, but also postcards, stuffed animals, bottle caps, stamps, autographs, thimbles . . ."

Marja, who had been taking notes, looked up. "Thimbles?"

"That's weird," Gavin said.

"Yeah, sort of," Mr. Truman agreed.

"But some collectors will collect anything and everything."

"I'm sorry that Aidan's dad thought you stole his box," Sam said. "But I guess we've finally solved our mystery."

"Only now we have another mystery," Gavin said. "The mystery of who put Aidan's box in the lost and found."

Sam sighed. He was glad they'd dug the box out of the lost-and-found closet and figured out who it belonged to. But did he really want to spend the next week—or month or year?—trying to figure out who stole it in the first place?

"Let's solve that mystery next week," Sam said. "Maybe for the rest of this week we could be an actual bird-watching club."

"That's a great idea, Sam!" Emily said. "Let's go outside right now and look for red-tailed hawks. My dad saw one yesterday when he was driving home from work."

"Okay," Sam agreed. "I just need to go grab something first."

The rest of the club members were over by the baseball field when Sam got outside. Everyone was looking up at the sky. Sam was curious about what they were looking at, but there was one thing he had to do before he could join them.

The fifth-grade soccer game was breaking up by the time Sam ran over to the field. Chris Gutentag was walking off the field with another kid, and he looked surprised when Sam called out his name.

"Do I know you?" he asked when Sam got closer. "Are you friends with my little sister or something?"

Sam held out the red jacket with the little soccer ball patch on it. "I think this is yours," he said. "And I think you put it in the lost and found because it smelled bad."

Chris Gutentag's cheeks turned red. "I don't know what you're talking about."

"The thing is," Sam continued, feeling a little shaky, "there's something you can do to make stuff stop stinking so much. It sounds weird, but if you wash stinky things with vinegar, it really works." He held the jacket out to Chris. "Really. Smell it."

Chris sighed. "You're crazy," he said, but he took the jacket from Sam and sniffed. His eyes widened. "Wow, that smells so much better than it used to!"

"So then it *is* your jacket, right?" Sam asked.

"Yeah," Chris said, looking at his feet. "And my parents won't buy me a new one, so I guess I should say thanks for making this one not stink so bad." He looked up at Sam. "I mean, it's really weird that you washed it for me, but—I don't know, it's sort of cool, too. So thanks."

Sam shrugged. "That's okay."

He wanted to tell Chris the whole story, about how he and his friends had this detective club and Sam had come up with the idea to search the lost and found for interesting things, and how Chris's jacket wasn't actually interesting but they knew it would make Mrs. Mason happy if they tried to find the owner of at least one jacket. But Chris Gutentag was already walking away, so Sam didn't say anything.

But as he ran over to meet the members of the World's Best Detective/Bird-Watching Club, he was feeling pretty good about his lost-and-found plan.

Chapter Seventeen

Sam the Man and the Lost-and-Found Plan

"So what are you going to do with your eight dollars and thirty-three cents?" Mr. Stockfish asked Sam that afternoon as they walked to Mrs. Kerner's house. "I think I should get part of it since I'm the one who helped you out of a jam."

"I guess so," Sam said. "We won't get our reward until next week though. Aidan said his dad would bring it to school on Monday and leave it with Mrs. Mason."

"Your club solved three mysteries in a row," Mr. Stockfish said. "That's an impressive record."

Sam stopped to scoop up a rock from the ground. It was gray and egg-shaped. Maybe it was a fossilized egg laid by an ancient bird on this spot two thousand years ago. Maybe it was laid by the first chicken that wasn't a dinosaur!

Probably not, but Sam would get Annabelle to help him do some research on the computer when he got home.

Doing research was a little bit like solving a mystery, Sam thought. He wouldn't mind being the sort of person who solved mysteries about fossils and dinosaurs.

"I don't know if I want to keep being a detective, at least the kind who solves crimes," Sam told Mr. Stockfish as he slipped the rock into his pocket. "I mean, sure, if there was a big case maybe. But there aren't a lot of big cases in elementary school. Most of the cases aren't really cases at all."

"I think the locked box was a big case," Mr. Stockfish said, leaning toward a bush to give it a sniff. "And you cracked it. Plus, you made eight dollars. I'm kidding about sharing it. I'm just glad I could help you out."

"Me too," Sam said. "For a minute I think Mr. Truman really thought we were criminals. We might have gotten kicked out of school. It was lucky you were home. You know what else is lucky?"

"What?"

"That kid who the box belonged to— Aidan? He collects stuffed animals. He was really excited when I told him about the snake in my garage."

"A lot more excited than your mother was when she tripped over it, I would assume," Mr. Stockfish said.

"Yeah, that wasn't good," Sam said. "Now there's a rule that I can't store anything in our garage without getting my parents' permission first."

"So what are you going to do with your money?" Mr. Stockfish asked again when they reached Mrs. Kerner's driveway. "Eight dollars isn't a whole lot, but it's not nothing."

Sam had been thinking about this all afternoon. He thought about starting a monster truck fund, so he could buy a monster truck when he was sixteen and had his driver's license. He thought about saving up for another chicken to add to Mrs. Kerner's flock. He also thought about spending it all on candy, although he had a feeling his mom and dad wouldn't like that idea very much.

"I was thinking if everyone in our club really wanted to become bird-watchers, we could put all of our money together," Sam said. "We could buy a pair of binoculars that Mrs. Haynie could keep in her desk. Then we'd have that pair and Marja's to look at birds with."

"I think that's a fine idea, Sam," said Mr. Stockfish. "Who knows, maybe you could use those binoculars for solving mysteries too." He paused to open the gate to Mrs. Kerner's backyard. "I think you should try to find out who stole that box in the first place."

"Maybe," Sam said. "It *is* the most mysterious-sounding mystery so far. But there aren't any clues."

They walked across Mrs. Kerner's backyard toward the chicken coop. "Maybe there aren't any clues, but there are some interesting questions," Mr. Stockfish said. "For instance, why did the person who stole the box put it in the lost and found?"

Sam thought about this. He had to admit, he liked how trying to figure stuff out was like working a puzzle. "Maybe nobody stole it," he said after a minute. "Maybe the box really got lost, but it wasn't until a week later that somebody found it and put it in the lost and found."

"An interesting theory, Sam the Man," Mr. Stockfish said as he reached into the chicken coop and pulled Leroy out. "Maybe you'll crack this case after all— you and your club, that is."

"Six heads are better than one," Sam agreed. "I wonder if there's ever been a six-headed chicken."

"I've heard of a two-headed chicken," Mr. Stockfish said as he sat down in his chair and set Leroy on his lap. "But not one with six heads."

When Sam went to check the chickens' water, he saw a small blue bird perched on top of the waterer. What kind of bird was it, he wondered? A blue jay? A plain old bluebird? Or were there other kinds of blue birds, ones that Sam had never heard of? Sam thought that maybe being a bird-watcher was a lot like being a detective. You made guesses, you asked questions, you talked to experts. Maybe you figured out the answer, maybe you didn't.

Either way, Sam thought, a pair of binoculars would come in handy.

Acknowledgments

Many thanks to the following folks: The ever-astonishing Caitlyn Dlouhy, the marvelous Alex Borbolla, and the wise and wonderful Justin Chanda.

A good copy editor is a writer's best friend: Thank you, Clare McGlade, for making my sentences the best they can be. Thanks to Sonia Chaghatzbanian for designing such beautiful books, and thanks to Tatyana Rosalia for making the Sam books shine. Finally, thanks to Amy Bates, whose wonderful illustrations bring Sam & Co. to life.

As always, I appreciate the forebearance and affection of my home team: Clifton, Jack, Will and Travis the Dog.

What will Sam plan next?
Find out in this sneak peek of
SAM THE MAN & the Cell Phone Plan!

SAM THE MAN
& the Cell Phone Plan

FRANCES O'ROARK DOWELL
Illustrated by Amy June Bates

Sam "Just the Facts" Graham

Sam Graham was an information man.

In his room he had three books about chickens, seven books about monster trucks, one copy of *Guinness World Records*, and a comic book called *Everything You Need to Know About the Solar System*.

When his second-grade class went to the library, Sam helped the other kids look things up on the computer. He helped

Emily find websites about bird calls, and he helped Will look up statistics on his favorite college football team. When Sam needed facts about his favorite food group, he knew the best thing to type into the search engine box was "frozen waffles history," because if he just typed "frozen waffles," all the hits would be commercials, and commercials never had facts in them.

Sam liked facts. He liked researching facts about interesting topics. He liked sharing the facts he learned with other people.

Which is why Sam Graham needed his very own phone.

"A phone? Why on earth does a second grader need a phone?" Sam's mom asked when Sam told her what he wanted for his birthday. She was sitting at the breakfast table, reading the newspaper on her laptop computer.

"I like looking things up," Sam said, taking a bite of his frozen waffle. "It would be nice if I could look up stuff while I was on the school bus or taking care of the chickens in Mrs. Kerner's backyard. And if I had a phone and there was a chicken emergency, I could call 9-1-1."

"You don't call 9-1-1 for chickens, Sam the Man," Sam's sister, Annabelle, told him. "You'd get in trouble if you did."

"Well, I could call you or Mom or Dad, then," Sam said. "Or the chicken hotline."

"Is there really a chicken hotline?"

Sam's mom asked, looking over her computer screen at Sam and Annabelle.

"If I had a phone, I could look it up and see," Sam said.

Annabelle took out her phone from her back pocket. "I'll check."

"No phones at the table, Annabelle," Sam's mom said. "You know the rules."

"But you have your laptop at the table," Annabelle pointed out. "That's almost the same as a phone."

"In this case, my laptop is really a newspaper," Sam's mom said. "So it's different."

"If I had a phone, I could read the paper too," Sam said. "My phone could be a newspaper or a book or an encyclopedia or a radio."

Sam's dad walked into the kitchen. He

had his phone in his hand and was texting someone.

"And I could text you if I had to stay late for school or needed to come home because I had a stomachache," Sam continued. "I could do a million things with a phone."

"You're too young for a phone, Sam the Man," Sam's dad said, putting *his* phone on the kitchen counter. "You spend too much time looking at screens as it is."

Sam poured some more syrup on his frozen waffle. "Why isn't Annabelle too young?" he asked.

"Annabelle is in sixth grade," Sam's dad said. "She has Scouts and soccer and swim team. She also has asthma, so it makes me and your mom feel better to know she can get in touch with us if she feels an attack coming on while she's at school or a game."

"Besides, Sam, you have lots of ways to look things up," Sam's mom added, closing her laptop and taking her plate to the sink. "You can use the computer in my office upstairs if I'm there to supervise, and you can always check out books from the

library. You don't need a phone to find things out."

Sam thought about this. He knew there were lots of ways to look up facts. But he couldn't take pictures using a book, and he couldn't pull his mom's computer out of his pocket if he needed to send someone a message. And what was he supposed to do if he had a chicken coop emergency? Throw eggs up into the air and hope someone came to see what was the matter?

But he could tell from their expressions that his parents weren't going to get him a phone for his birthday, even if it *was* the best idea ever. The problem, Sam thought as he scrubbed syrup off his arm with his napkin, was now all he could think about was how much he wanted a phone. How much he *needed* a phone. How he would never be happy until the day he finally had a phone of his own.

There was only one thing to do. Sam would have to come up with a plan.

He tried to come up with one while he was brushing his teeth. Maybe he could ask Annabelle if he could rent her phone part time, even though he knew she'd probably say no. Annabelle was the kind of sister who would help you out, but she wouldn't break the rules for you.

He could look in the school lost and found to see if anyone had lost a phone. Sure, he'd have to give the phone back to its owner, but maybe that person would be so happy that Sam had found their phone, they'd let Sam use it whenever he wanted. They might even let Sam bring it home on the weekends.

Sam liked that plan a lot, but his parents probably wouldn't.

By the time Sam had finished brushing his teeth, put on his jacket, and walked to the bus stop, he'd thought of six different plans, but he was pretty sure none of them would work.

Sam wasn't used to coming up with bad plans. It made him feel dumb. It was like when he played T-ball last spring and kept hitting the tee instead of the ball when it was his turn to bat.

"You look sad, Sam," Sam's best friend, Gavin, said when he got to the bus stop. "Did you lose something?"

Sam shook his head. "I'm trying to come up with a plan for getting a phone, but I can't think of anything good."

"No one in second grade has a phone," Gavin said. "Well, Hutch did for a little while, remember? His mom put tracking devices in his jacket and lunch box because Hutch was always losing them. He was supposed to use the phone to track his lost stuff."

"But he lost the phone," Sam said, nodding. "I remember."

"I don't think you need a phone," Gavin said. "But if you really want one, you could tell your parents you'd pay for it. You're good at making money."

"I still don't think they'd let me have one," Sam said.

"So then why are you trying to come up with a plan to get one?" Gavin asked.

Sam saw the bus coming down the street and picked up his backpack. "I don't know. I just really want a phone."

"I feel the same way about cats," Gavin said, lining up with Sam for the bus. "I really, really want a cat. But I'm allergic to cats, and so is everybody else in my family. So I'm never going to have a cat, even though I want one more than anything."

"No one is my family is allergic to phones," Sam said. "In fact, I'm the only person who doesn't have one. It's not fair."

"Life's not fair," Gavin said as they stepped onto the bus. "Otherwise I wouldn't have a cat allergy."

"I guess," Sam said. He was about to say something else when he slipped on a piece of paper on the bus floor. He didn't fall, but he did bump into the boy in front of him.

The boy turned around and said, "Watch it!" He was carrying a box, which he showed to Sam. "I made a robot for the third-grade science fair, and I don't want to break it."

"Sorry," Sam said. He wished he could peek inside the box to see what the boy's robot looked like. He wondered if it would be hard to make a robot, one that walked and talked and did all kinds of interesting things. Maybe next year Sam would make his own robot for the science fair.

Or—

Sam turned around to Gavin. "I've got it! I've come up with a plan!"

"What is it?" Gavin asked.

"I'm going to make my own phone!" Sam told him. "It's going to be great!"

"Make a phone?" Gavin sounded confused. "How do you *make* a phone?"

Sam shrugged. "I don't know. But I know how to look it up."

If there was one thing Sam was good at, it was looking things up.

Looking for another great book?
Find it
IN THE MIDDLE.

Fun, fantastic books for kids
in the in-be**TWEEN** age.

InTheMiddleBooks.com

Meet the Chicken Squad: Dirt, Sugar, Poppy, and Sweetie.

These **chicks** are *not* your typical barnyard puffs of fluff. . . . No, they're too busy solving mysteries and fighting crime. No mystery is too big or too small for the Chicken Squad—at least THEY don't think so.